ARE
MONSTERS
SCARY?

WRITTEN BY:
CAMERON EITTREIM

RD Publishing INC.
P.O. Box 180733
FORT SMITH AR 72908
www.rdpublishing.org

Ordering Information:
Quantity sales. Special discounts are available on quantity purchases by corporations, associations, and others. For details, contact the publisher at the address above.
Orders by U.S. trade bookstores and wholesalers. Please contact Lulu Distribution: Tel: 1 844-212-0689.; Fax: 1-888-265-2129 or visit www.lulu.com.

Printed in the United States of America

Cataloging-in-Publication data

Eittreim, Cameron.
Are Monsters Scary? : Cameron Eittreim.
p. cm.
ISBN: 978-1-387-76022-0
1. Children's.
I. Johnson, Ben. II. Managing Director.
HF0000.A0 A00 2010
299.000 00–dc22 2010999999

First Edition

14 13 12 11 10 / 10 9 8 7 6 5 4 3 2 1

[this page intentionally left blank]

Acknowledgement

I'd like to acknowledge everyone in life who has given me a second chance, even when the odds were stacked against me. Everything I do is show my kids that you can do whatever you want in this life. You can work for yourself, you don't always need to go to college, and you can do anything you put your mind to, just like me.

Dedication

This book is dedicated to my kids. There is nothing better in life than being your dad, and nothing else in the world will replace it. I don't need money, a great job, or anything else in life as long as I have you. Hope you like this book. I interviewed many scary monsters for you guys.

- Love Dad.

1

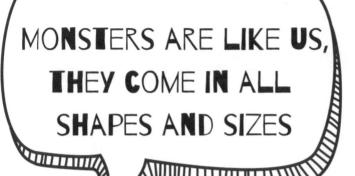

3

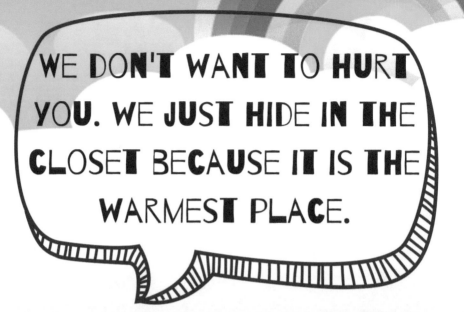

GETTING BACK HOME THROUGH THE TIME PORTAL IS ALMOST IMPOSSIBLE. SO MOST MONSTERS MAKE A HOME IN YOUR CLOSET.

6

YOUR MONSTER FRIENDS ALSO HAVE VERY **FUN BIRTHDAY** PARTIES **WITH** EACH OTHER. THE MONSTER IN YOUR ROOM MIGHT BE YOUNGER **THEN YOU!**

SPACE IS SO FUN AND THERE IS SO MUCH TO SEE AND DO. ALL IF YOU USE YOUR IMAGINATION.

12

THE SKY IS THE LIMIT AS TO THE AMOUNT OF FUN THAT YOU CAN HAVE WITH YOUR MONSTER FRIENDS. JUST USE YOUR IMAGINATION AND THE SKY WILL OPEN.

14

MONSTER ISLAND IS A FUN PLACE TO USE YOUR IMAGINATION TO GET TO AS WELL.

16

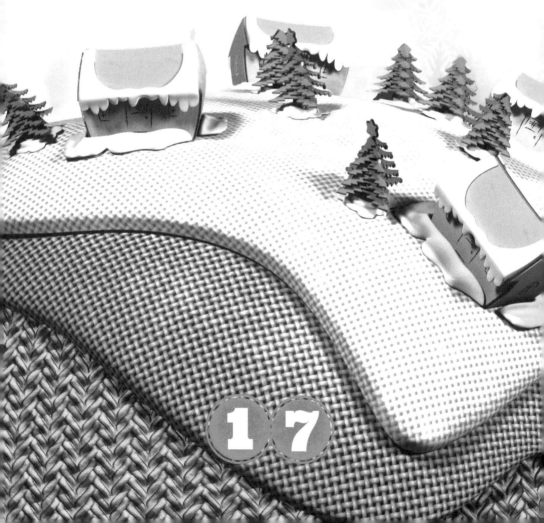

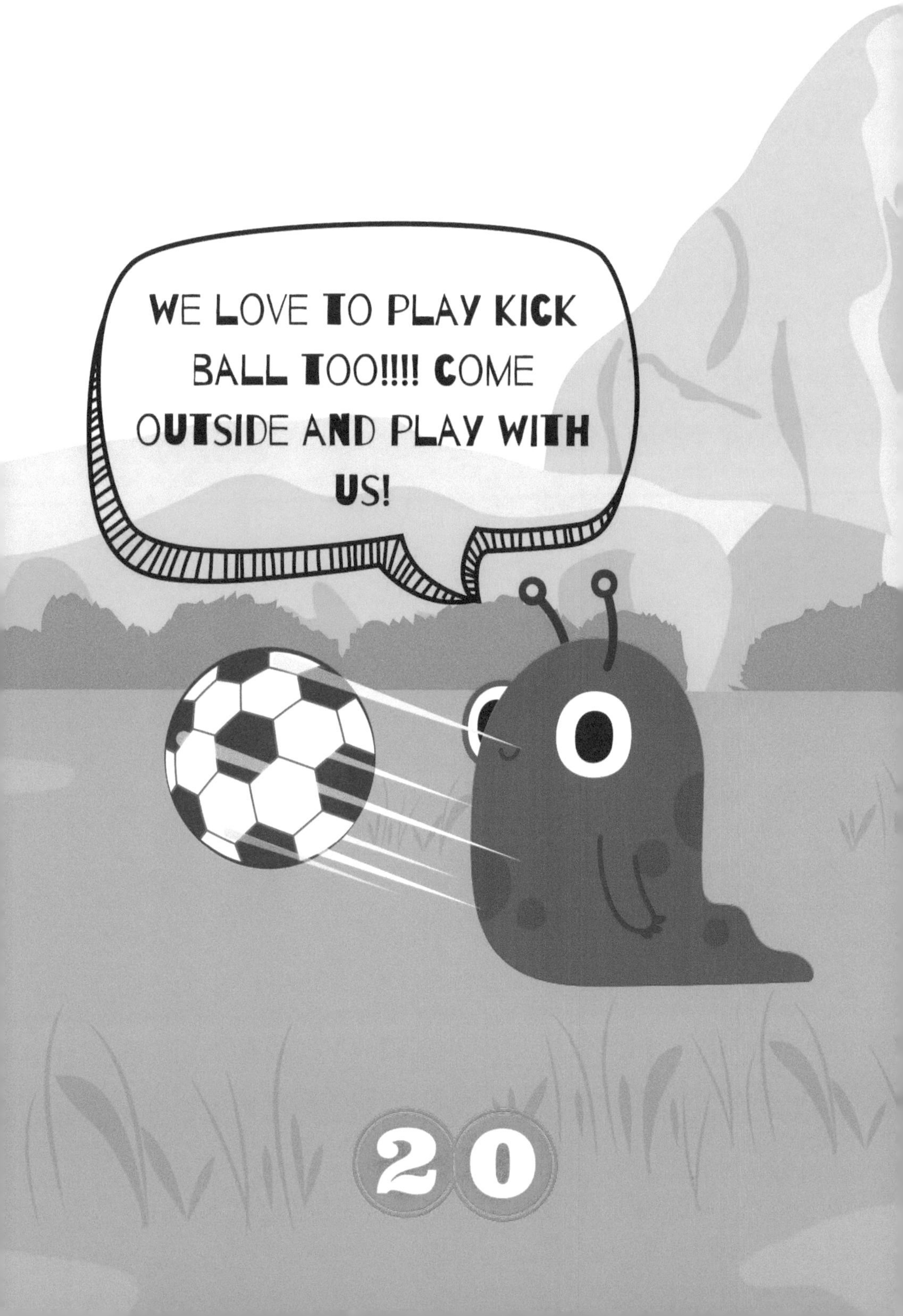
WE LOVE TO PLAY KICK BALL TOO!!!! COME OUTSIDE AND PLAY WITH US!

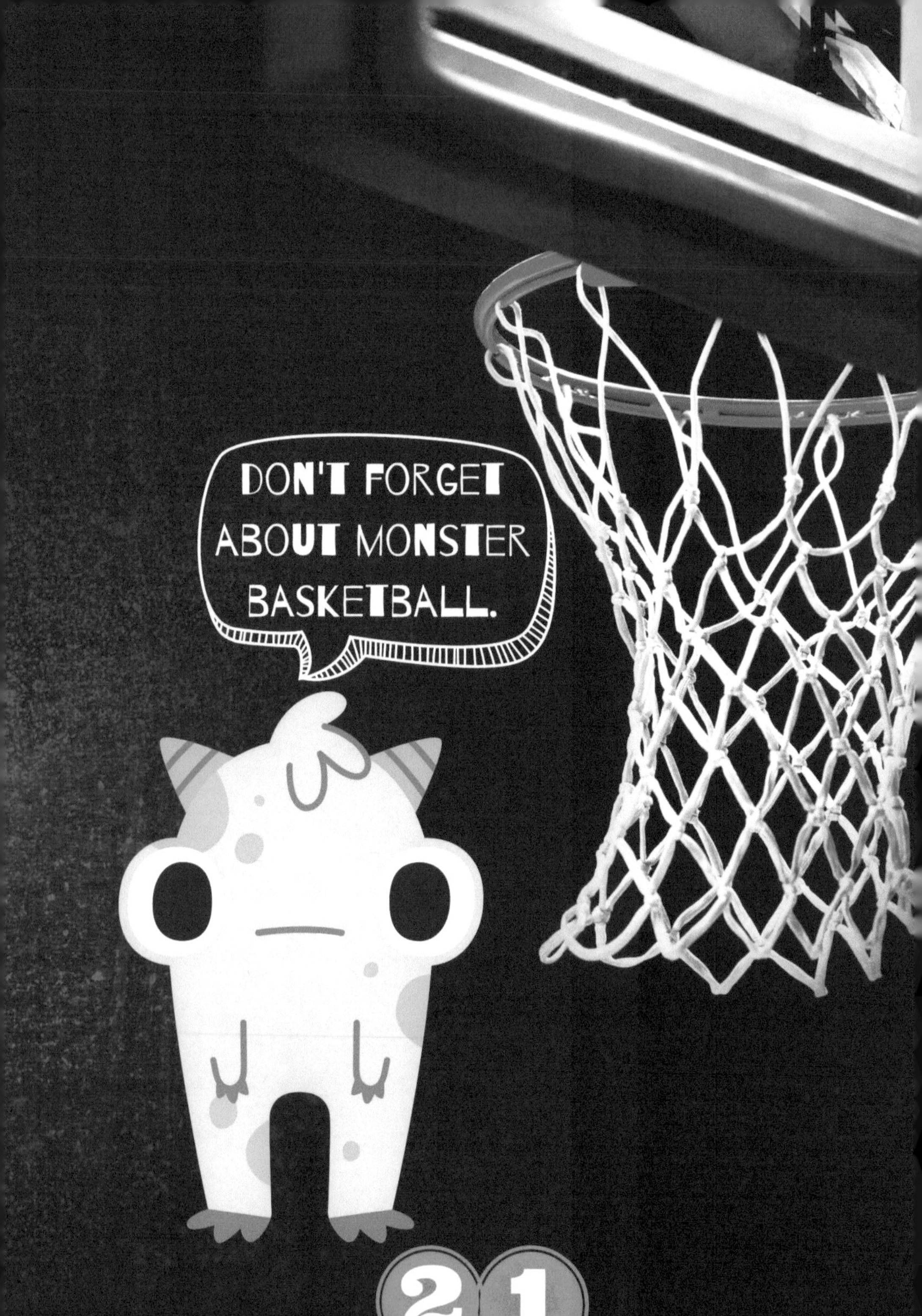
DON'T FORGET ABOUT MONSTER BASKETBALL.

WHEN YOU STOP BEING AFRAID OF MONSTERS YOU WILL HAVE SO MUCH FUN.

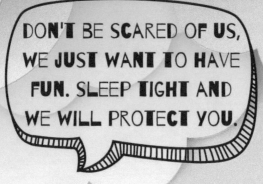

25

ABOUT THE AUTHOR

Cameron Eittreim is a Fort Smith, Arkansas based author who has published three books so far. He has been a writer since 2006, starting freelancing and eventually being published in some of the most well known entities in the world.

Cameron's work has been featured in Taste of Home Magazine, Life Wire, Dot Dash, SuperJump Magazine, Motor Junkie, Auto Wise, The Things, and many more publications. Cameron has also been a career bail bondsman and went from being homeless to one of the most well known bail agents in the California bail bonds industry.

He currently owns a commercial cleaning company, in addition to continuing his writing career and hosting a popular podcast radio show. More of his work can be seen at http://cameroneittreim.com/